Jack and Santa's
Frosty Fallout

# Jack and Santa's Frosty Fallout

Ian McEwan 2024

© 2024 Ian McEwan . All rights reserved.

No part of this book may be reproduced, distributed, or transmitted in any form or by any means, including photocopying, recording, or other electronic or mechanical methods, without the prior written permission of the publisher, except in the case of brief quotations embodied in critical reviews and certain other non-commercial uses permitted by copyright law.

Ian McEwan  asserts the moral right to be identified as the author of this work.

This is a work of fiction. Names, characters, places, and incidents are either the product of the author's imagination or used fictitiously. Any resemblance to actual persons, living or dead, events, or locales is entirely coincidental.

Published by:
Independently published

# Table of Contents

# Jack and Santa's Frosty Fallout

## Chapter 1: Introduction

In the snowy, twinkling North Pole, the elves were in overdrive. With only five days left until Christmas, Santa's workshop buzzed with frantic energy. Bells jingled from the rafters as elves hurried from one task to the next, their small hands a blur of motion as they wrapped, painted, and assembled toys. But beneath the joyful hustle, a sense of urgency crackled in the air.

Santa, however, was more flustered than ever.

"Only five days left!" Santa muttered, his pacing so fast it left tracks in the glittering snow-dusted floor. His rosy cheeks, normally a jolly pink, had turned a deep crimson, flushed with worry. "The sleigh's still broken, the naughty and nice list is a mess, and the satellite tracker is completely out of date!" He paused, staring at the ceiling as if the stars might hold the answers. "How am I supposed to get everything done in time?"

He ran a gloved hand through his snow-white beard, "In all my centuries of Christmases, I've never been this far behind," Santa thought, his chest tightening. The weight of the season felt heavier this year, like a snowfall that refused to let up. His hands trembled, hidden beneath his thick gloves. Was this the year it would all fall apart? What would happen if the children woke up to find nothing under their trees? No gifts. No magic. No Christmas. The thought gnawed at him. He had seen the world through so many dark times, brought joy in the face of war, famine, even pandemics. But this... this chaos in his own workshop, his own home, was something different. "Maybe I'm losing my touch," he muttered under his breath. "Maybe this is all just too much."

The elves, sensing his distress, scrambled even harder. One team hovered around the sleigh, tightening bolts and replacing worn-out runners. Another group worked feverishly to update the naughty and nice book, sorting through names with furrowed brows as they cross-checked against their glowing scrolls. Others were huddled over maps and gadgets, recalibrating the satellite tracker that helped Santa navigate the ever-growing number of homes around the world.

Still, despite their best efforts, everything felt like it was teetering on the edge of chaos.

"Careful with that!" Santa called out as a stack of wrapped gifts wobbled precariously, threatening to topple. "We can't afford any more—"

But before he could finish, a sharp gust of icy wind blew through the workshop, scattering papers and snuffing out candles. The elves froze, their pointy ears twitching in the sudden chill. The temperature dropped in an instant, colder than any North Pole winter.

Santa's heart sank. He knew this kind of cold.

A figure glided in on the gust, his presence unmistakable:

Jack Frost. His pale blue skin shimmered like frozen glass, and his frostbitten smile curled at the corners as he slid effortlessly across the icy floor. Snowflakes danced around him, glittering in the dim light of the workshop.

"Well, well, well," Jack said, his voice sharp as ice cracking over a frozen lake. "Looks like someone's in a bit of a bind."

The elves stepped back nervously, their busy hands suddenly still. Even Santa, who was no stranger to handling Christmas crises, felt his stomach tighten. Jack Frost was as unpredictable as winter itself—sometimes playful, other times downright troublesome. And right now, Santa didn't have time for games.

"Jack," Santa said, his voice stern but controlled, "this really isn't a good time."

Jack's grin widened. "Oh, I know. That's what makes it so much fun."

He stepped forward, trailing a finger along a nearby candy cane, which immediately frosted over at his touch. "You know, Santa, I've always wondered—what happens if Christmas doesn't come together in time?" Jack's eyes sparkled with mischief. "What if the sleigh doesn't fly? What if the gifts aren't delivered?"

Santa squared his shoulders, determination flickering behind his tired eyes. "Christmas will happen," he said, more to himself than to Jack.

But even as he spoke, doubt lingered in the frosty air.

A Special Christmas Adventure

In another part of the world...

A little girl named Sophie, and her brother Tom were em-
barking on the adventure of a lifetime. As a special surprise, their parents had whisked them away to the magical
land of Lapland just before Christmas. Snow blanketed the
earth in soft, powdery drifts, and the air smelled of pine
and chimney smoke, carrying a kind of crisp excitement
that only the holiday season could bring.

For Sophie, though, the trip held an extra layer of impor-
tance. Her birthday was on Christmas Day—a day that
should have felt as special as it sounded, but rarely did.

"Can you imagine, Tom?" Sophie said, pulling her knitted
scarf tighter as snowflakes danced like tiny stars around
them. Her breath puffed out in small clouds, her voice
tinged with a mix of wonder and frustration. "A birthday
on Christmas Day! It's like everyone forgets it's my birthday, too. They only care about Christmas."

Tom, a year younger and endlessly excitable, wasn't paying
much attention. His eyes were fixed on something far more
interesting. "Yeah, but look! We get to ride a real sleigh!"
he shouted, pointing at the large wooden sleigh waiting for
them a few feet away. It was already hitched to a powerful
reindeer, its broad chest covered in jingling silver bells that
sparkled in the waning light.

Sophie glanced over and tried to suppress her own excitement. Despite her complaints, the sight of the sleigh—straight out of a storybook—was too magical to ignore. She climbed in with her brother, their feet sinking into the thick, fur-lined seats.

"We'll be right behind you," their mother reassured them, pulling her coat tight as she and their father helped them settle in.

But just as their parents turned to climb into the sleigh themselves, the reindeer let out a loud, excited snort. It pawed the snow, nostrils flaring, eyes wide and gleaming with an energy that wasn't there moments before. Before anyone could react, the sleigh jolted forward with a sudden, powerful lurch.

"Wait!" their father called, but the words were swallowed by the wind as the reindeer galloped ahead, tearing through the snow. Sophie and Tom's shouts of surprise quickly turned into gasps of fear as they clutched the sides of the sleigh, holding on for dear life.

Trees rushed past in a blur, the world becoming a dizzying mix of white, green, and the brown of pine trunks. The wind stung their faces, sharp and cold, and the sleigh bounced wildly over the uneven ground. Sophie's heart raced in her chest. "Tom! What's happening?!"

"I don't know!" Tom's voice wavered between excitement and terror, his fingers gripping the edge of the sleigh so tightly his knuckles turned white.

Then something strange happened. The sleigh seemed to lose contact with the snow for a second—just a heartbeat—and then again, for longer. The ground below began to blur as if it were pulling away from them.

"We're... we're flying!" Sophie gasped, eyes wide with disbelief.

Up, up, and up they went, the reindeer's strong legs no longer touching the snow as it soared into the air, pulling the sleigh behind it. The snowy forest, once a maze of towering trees, was now far below them. The treetops looked like patches of frost on the landscape, growing smaller with each passing second.

Tom's fear seemed to melt away, replaced with pure awe. "Look, Sophie! We're flying! We're really flying!" He leaned over the side, laughing despite the rush of wind that whipped around them.

Sophie, though still clutching the edge of the sleigh, couldn't help but smile. She watched as the world below transformed into a sprawling winter wonderland—one that seemed too perfect, too magical to be real.

Yet here they were, rising higher into the sky, carried off into the unknown by a reindeer that wasn't just pulling a sleigh—it was pulling them into something far more extraordinary.

## Chapter 2: Back at the North Pole

Meanwhile, back at the North Pole, the usually cheery

workshop was teetering on the edge of chaos. Jack Frost was up to his usual tricks, and with each mischievous step, he left behind glistening patches of ice that sent elves—and productivity—spiraling.

Jack darted from corner to corner, an impish grin plastered on his face, as he slid past a group of elves carrying boxes of toys. The elves' pointy shoes slipped on the sudden frost, sending them tumbling into a heap of brightly wrapped presents. Glittering ribbons, bows, and ornaments flew through the air like confetti.

"Oops!" Jack cackled, not even bothering to hide his amusement. He pirouetted across the floor, leaving a trail of ice that shimmered under the workshop lights.

Santa, sitting with his leg propped up after an earlier fall, watched the scene unfold with growing frustration. His usually jolly face was clouded, and his once twinkling eyes now narrowed in irritation. "Jack, this is no time for your tricks!" he boomed, rubbing his sore leg. "We've got too much to do, and Christmas is only four days away!"

But Jack just grinned, sliding effortlessly between the bustling elves, who were doing their best to stay on task despite the frozen hazards underfoot. "Oh, come on, Santa!" Jack said, his voice as smooth as a freshly iced pond. "What's Christmas without a little fun?" He snapped his fingers, and frost crept up the windows, coating them in intricate icy patterns that sparkled like diamonds in the soft glow of the workshop.

Santa groaned, feeling the weight of the holiday season heavier than ever. The elves, trying to keep up with their already towering workloads, were constantly interrupted by Jack's antics. One slipped on an ice patch as he rushed with a tray of freshly made cookies, the treats flying through the air and landing with a splat across the floor. Another tripped over a patch of frost as he tried to deliver a sack of gifts, spilling toys everywhere like confetti from an overturned box.

Santa rubbed his temples, the pounding in his head competing with the endless jingling of bells in the workshop. "Jack," he said slowly, trying to keep his temper in check, "I'm warning you. This is serious business! There's no room for distractions!"

Jack, however, was unfazed. His grin widened as he zipped around the room, sending a cascade of frost along the workshop floor. "Serious?" he mocked, skating backward without missing a beat. "Where's the fun in that?"

## Chapter 3: The Trouble Escalates

As Jack continued to spread ice and chaos with reckless abandon, the elves found themselves in an ever-growing winter obstacle course. They tiptoed cautiously, their feet slipping on the frosty floor as they tried to balance toy-making and gift-wrapping with the new task of not falling on their faces.

Santa's patience was wearing thin. He watched, grim-faced, as his team struggled just to stay upright, let alone meet their tight deadlines. "Jack, enough is enough!" Santa bellowed, his voice booming through the workshop. "There's no time for games!"

But Jack was in no mood to listen. With a playful smirk, he skated up to Santa's desk and, with a dramatic flourish, summoned an extra-large patch of ice directly in Santa's path. It was a move meant to amuse, to rile up the big guy, but Jack had no idea just how much damage it would cause.

"Santa! Watch out!" cried a nearby elf, his voice cracking with panic as his small arms flailed in alarm. But it was too late.

Santa, his thoughts consumed by the mountain of tasks left undone, pushed himself off his chair, his mind too focused on fixing the sleigh to notice the dangerous gleam of ice beneath his boots. He took one determined step—and the ground betrayed him.

His foot hit the ice, and for one awful moment, time seemed to slow. Santa's eyes widened as he felt himself lose balance, his legs sliding out from under him in a blur of red velvet. He reached out instinctively, but there was nothing to grab. The cold hit him before the floor did, pain blooming through his leg like a sharp frost creeping up his spine.

The workshop fell silent as the sound of Santa hitting the ground echoed. Elves rushed forward, their tiny hands trembling as they knelt beside him. Santa groaned, clutching his leg, feeling the weight of the holiday season grow heavier.

"Jack Frost!" Santa roared, his voice shaking with frustration. His normally rosy cheeks flushed crimson. "Look what you've done!"

Jack, hovering nearby, simply shrugged. "Hey, it's not my fault you weren't paying attention," he said, twirling a snowflake between his fingers with a smirk. "I was just having a bit of fun."

Santa, now propped up by his loyal elves, his leg suspended in a sling of festive red fabric, had finally had enough. His eyes, usually kind and full of warmth, were now cold with irritation. "That's it, Jack!" Santa thundered, pointing toward the door. "You're done here. Leave the North Pole—now!"

Jack's grin faltered for a moment, his icy blue eyes narrowing in disbelief. He puffed out his chest, trying to regain his cocky demeanor. "Fine! If you think you can handle Christmas without me, go ahead and try!" His voice crackled with a mix of pride and anger, but beneath it, there was the slightest hint of hurt.

Santa: "You've caused enough trouble, Jack. What do you really want?"

Jack: "What do I want? Oh, Santa. Isn't it obvious? I've always been in the background, haven't I? You get the songs, the stories, the admiration. And I? I'm just a footnote. The cold snap. The chill in the air. But this time... this year... they'll see. They'll see that winter's true power doesn't come from you, but from me. And when Christmas fails? They'll have no choice but to turn to me."

With one last glance around the chaotic workshop, Jack turned sharply on his heel and stomped toward the exit, leaving a trail of frost in his wake. He threw open the door, a gust of cold air rushing in as he stormed out into the snowy night, slamming it shut behind him.

For a long moment, no one spoke. The elves stood frozen, watching the door with wide eyes, unsure of what to do. Santa, breathing heavily, let out a tired sigh as he sank back into his chair. His leg was injured, Jack was gone, and there were only four days left until Christmas.

"We've got a lot of work to do," Santa muttered, rubbing his temples once more. The elves nodded, slowly returning to their tasks, but the festive mood had been replaced with a tense sense of urgency.

As the workshop creaked back into motion, Santa gazed out the frost-covered window. Somewhere, in the darkness beyond, Jack Frost was out there—angry, unpredictable, and dangerous. And with Christmas hanging by a thread, the North Pole was going to need more than just holiday magic to save the day.

## Chapter 4: All Hell Breaks Loose

No sooner had the door slammed shut behind Jack Frost than flashing red lights erupted throughout the North Pole. A shrill, piercing alarm echoed through the halls, causing every elf in Santa's workshop to freeze in place, eyes wide with confusion and dread. Santa himself bolted upright in his chair, his injured leg momentarily forgotten.

"What in blazes is going on?" Santa growled, scanning the chaotic workshop. His heart pounded as the alarm's shriek grew louder, filling every corner of the North Pole with urgency.

"Unauthorized landing! Incoming without permission!" an elf near the control tower shouted, pointing toward the sky.

Santa squinted through the frost-covered window and felt his stomach drop. Cutting through the swirling snowstorm, a familiar glow pulsed in the night—a bright, unmistakable red light piercing the dark sky.

"Rudolph?" Santa's voice was barely above a whisper, his heart sinking like a stone. "What on earth is happening now?"

Before he could gather his thoughts, instinct kicked in. Santa barked out orders with military precision. "Man the landing stations! Fire team elves on standby! Snickel, get your team into position—NOW!"

Snickel, the lead elf, didn't waste a second. He sprinted toward the runway, his team of elves racing behind him, their tiny boots crunching through the deep snow. The sleigh was already visible in the distance, its silhouette wobbling and jerking through the sky. "It's Rudolph, alright!" Snickel called out, squinting at the approaching chaos. "But there's no one flying the sleigh! He's coming in blind!"

Santa's despair deepened. He gripped the arms of his chair, the tendons in his hand tight with stress. "What else could possibly go wrong tonight?" he muttered under his breath, feeling the weight of the holiday season crushing down on him.

The elves rushed to their posts, waving glowing wands and signaling to the reindeer, but Rudolph was coming in fast, the sleigh swaying wildly behind him. He didn't slow down. In a split second, the sleigh slammed into the snowy runway with a deafening thud, skidding and spinning across the ice. Elves dove out of the way as the sleigh careened past, scattering mounds of snow in its wake.

"Look out!" a voice rang out, but it was too late. The sleigh crashed into a neatly stacked pile of presents, toppling them like a house of cards. Toys, ribbons, and wrapping paper spilled everywhere.

Santa groaned, slumping back in his chair. "What in the world is happening now? Who's in that sleigh?"

Snickel, panting from the sprint, approached the wrecked sleigh cautiously. As the snow and smoke cleared, he stopped dead in his tracks, his eyes widening in shock. Two small figures sat huddled in the sleigh, holding on for dear life—wide-eyed and terrified.

"Santa," Snickel shouted over the wind, "you'd better come see this!"

Sophie and Tom clung to each other in the sleigh, their knuckles white from the grip. Their hearts thundered in their chests, the wind whipping their faces raw. The sleigh skidded violently across the icy ground, the world a blur of white and flashing lights. It felt like forever until the sleigh finally crashed into a pile of gifts, sending them tumbling and jerking to a stop.

For a long moment, neither of them moved.

Sophie peeked over the edge of the sleigh, her breath shaky. "Tom... are we... are we alive?"

Tom, still gripping the side of the sleigh with trembling hands, nodded numbly. "I think so... but... where are we?"

They looked around, eyes wide with confusion and awe. Blinking against the harsh glow of warning lights and the flurry of activity surrounding them, they could make out dozens of small figures running toward them through the snow, their green-and-red uniforms and pointy hats bouncing as they moved.

Sophie's eyes widened as the figures came into focus. "Tom... are those... elves?"

Before Tom could answer, the lead elf reached them. His tiny, serious face peered up at them from beneath his snow-dusted hat. "Are you kids alright?" he asked, his voice both stern and gentle, trying to assess the situation.

Sophie nodded quickly, too stunned to speak. Tom nodded as well, still gripping the sleigh's edge like it might suddenly take off again.

Just then, a deep, booming voice echoed across the snow-covered runway, cutting through the noise. "What is going on here?"

Sophie and Tom whipped their heads toward the voice. Through the swirling snow, a large figure emerged, flanked by elves on either side, guiding him carefully across the icy ground. His red suit was unmistakable, his long white beard blowing gently in the wind. It was him—Santa Claus.

Sophie's heart skipped a beat. "Tom... is that... is that, Santa?"

Tom could only stare, his mouth agape, unable to believe his eyes. They had crash-landed in the North Pole—and Santa Claus himself was walking toward them.

Santa's face was lined with concern, his usually jolly expression replaced by one of deep worry. "How in the world did they get here?" he muttered, rubbing his temples as he gazed at the wrecked sleigh. He turned to Snickel, his voice a mixture of frustration and confusion. "And where is Jack Frost when you need him?"

Sophie, despite her fear, finally found her voice. "We... we didn't mean to cause any trouble, Mr. Santa," she stammered. "We were just on a sleigh ride, and suddenly it took off by itself! We didn't know what was happening!"

Santa's stern face softened as he looked down at the two children, taking in their wide-eyed terror and trembling hands. His heart melted, seeing how frightened they were.

"Well now," Santa said, stroking his beard thoughtfully. "It seems we've got quite the situation on our hands, don't we?"

He turned to Snickel. "Get these kids inside where it's warm," Santa ordered. "And get that sleigh checked out. We need answers, and we need them fast."

The elves quickly surrounded Sophie and Tom, helping them out of the sleigh and guiding them through the snow toward the warmth of the workshop. Sophie glanced back over her shoulder as she walked, watching Santa oversee the cleanup of the wreckage.

"Tom," she whispered, her voice shaking with both awe and fear. "We... we're in the North Pole."

Tom, his face still pale, nodded slowly. "Yeah... but why do I get the feeling things are about to get even crazier?"

## Chapter 5: Back to Jack

While the storm he had summoned raged on outside, Jack Frost paced restlessly in his icy cave. The walls shimmered with the eerie blue glow of his magic, reflecting his simmering anger. His footsteps echoed, sending faint bursts of frost spiraling into the air with every frustrated wave of his hand. Icicles, long and jagged, hung from the cave's ceiling, growing ever longer as his irritation spiked.

"I can't believe Santa thinks he can do this without me," Jack grumbled, his voice cold and sharp as a winter wind. He flicked his fingers, and a new cascade of icicles formed, glistening like fangs above him. "All these years of making winter magical, and what do I get? Blamed for a little slip-up. As if anyone could keep their balance on that much ice!"

Outside, the storm grew fiercer, the winds howling like a pack of wild wolves. Snow swirled in a frenzy, piling higher and higher, burying anything that stood in its path. The once gentle flurries had transformed into an unforgiving blizzard, the kind that could grind the entire North Pole to a halt.

Jack stomped his foot, and the ground beneath him cracked, sending shock-waves of frost radiating out from his icy lair. Snow hissed and hissed, as if mirroring his emotions, coating the world in white.

Let Santa deal with that, Jack thought bitterly. His pride, his frustration—it all boiled to the surface, fueling the blizzard with relentless fury. He wasn't ready to let go of his anger. Not yet. Santa needed to see just how much he depended on him. Jack Frost wasn't some sideshow—he was the one who made winter winter. He was the chill in the air, the frost on the windows, the shimmer on every snowflake. Without him, what was Christmas but a cold, dull day?

But even as the storm reached its peak, a quiet unease began to gnaw at him. Jack paused mid-stride, his eyes narrowing as he stared through the mouth of his cave into the whirling snow beyond. The wind shrieked outside, bending the trees and blowing drifts of snow into towering walls. Yet, beneath the rage, there was a flicker of something softer. A memory, maybe. A reminder.

Winter was supposed to be magical, wasn't it?

He knew, deep down, that he didn't want to ruin Christmas. As much as he loved the cold, as much as he reveled in the sharp bite of frost, it was the joy of it all that made it worthwhile. The laughter of children building snowmen, the way the first snowflake lit up a person's face, the sparkle in the air that filled even the darkest night with hope.

Without that magic, what was winter? What was Jack Frost?

He folded his arms, staring at the swirling chaos outside, wrestling with himself. The storm outside wasn't just a display of his power—it was a reflection of his own turmoil. He'd wanted to teach Santa a lesson, to show him how much he was needed, but now that the blizzard was out of control, a doubt crept into his chest, chilling even him.

Jack's blue eyes flickered, the frosty light dimming slightly. "Let's see how they handle this without me," he muttered, though his voice had lost some of its icy bite. He hated to admit it, but part of him was curious—how long could the North Pole really function without Jack Frost?

But as he watched the snow thicken, his arms still crossed, he couldn't shake the unease twisting inside him. He didn't want to be the villain. Not really. He just wanted to be appreciated.

The blizzard outside howled on, relentless and cold. Jack stood there, arms wrapped tight around himself, gazing into the storm he'd created. The snow piled high, and the winds shrieked louder, but within his icy cave, Jack felt the first crack of hesitation.

## Chapter 6: The Search for Jack

Sophie and Tom sat quietly by the crackling fire in Santa's workshop, but despite the warmth radiating from the flames and the comfort of the carrot soup in their bellies, neither of them could shake the gnawing sense of guilt that had settled in their chests. The storm outside raged louder, shaking the windows, and with every howl of the wind, they felt the weight of it pressing down harder.

"We caused this," Sophie whispered, her voice barely audible over the popping embers. She stared into the flames, her mind racing. "The storm, the sleigh, everything... it's our fault."

Tom looked up, his brow furrowed in confusion. "What do you mean? We didn't do anything."

Sophie shook her head, her determination hardening. "Maybe not directly. But we were the ones in that sleigh. We got caught up in all this, and now Christmas is on the verge of being cancelled because of us. We can't just sit here and do nothing."

Tom hesitated, his spoon hovering over his bowl. "But what can we do?"

Sophie stood abruptly, her shadow flickering against the wall as she began pacing the room. Her eyes glinted with a growing resolve. "Jack Frost is causing the storm, right? Maybe if we find him and talk to him, we can convince him to stop. If he understood how important Christmas is to us—to everyone—maybe he'd change his mind."

Tom blinked, doubt creeping into his voice. "But... how would we even find Jack Frost? It's not like we know where he lives."

Sophie didn't answer right away, her gaze sweeping the room as if searching for an answer. Her eyes finally landed on a small desk in the corner, cluttered with papers and maps. Without a word, she marched over, rifling through the drawers with a sense of urgency. "There has to be something here," she muttered, tossing aside papers. "A clue... a map... something."

Tom watched, unsure, as she rummaged through the mess. The storm outside seemed to howl even louder, as if urging them to hurry. Finally, Sophie's fingers brushed against something brittle and old. She pulled it free, her heart skipping a beat.

"Tom!" she gasped, holding up a crinkled, yellowed map. The edges were torn and worn, but it was still legible. "Look! A map of the North Pole... and right here," she pointed, her finger hovering over a small marking beyond the snowy mountains, "there's Jack's cave!"

Tom scrambled over, his breath catching in his throat.

Sure enough, the map laid out a detailed view of the North Pole—Santa's workshop, the reindeer stables, the candy cane forest—and, in a far, remote part of the map, beyond a range of jagged mountains, was a small cave marked "Jack Frost."

Tom's eyes widened. "You're not serious." He looked at her, incredulous. "We can't just go out there! It's a full-on blizzard! We'll freeze before we even make it halfway!"

Sophie's face was set with determination. "We have to try. If we can talk to Jack, maybe we can stop all of this. We can fix it, Tom. We can save Christmas."

Tom bit his lip, staring out the frosted window. The wind screamed against the panes, shaking the glass. He knew Sophie was right, but the idea of venturing out into the heart of the storm terrified him.

Still, as he glanced back at his sister's resolute expression, something inside him shifted. Sophie had always been braver than him—always the first to take a leap, while he hesitated. He swallowed hard and nodded. "Alright. Let's go."

They wasted no time. The two children bundled themselves up in the thickest, warmest clothes they could find, piling on scarves, hats, and mittens. Sophie carefully folded the old map and tucked it into her coat pocket, keeping it safe and dry.

With one last look around the cozy room, they slipped out of the door, unnoticed by the busy elves who were too preoccupied with trying to salvage Christmas. The cold hit them instantly, biting at their faces, but they pushed forward, pulling their hoods tight.

The storm was a beast. The wind howled ferociously, whipping snow into their faces, and the world around them was a swirl of white. The snowdrifts were high, and their progress was slow, but Sophie kept her eyes on the distant mountains, her determination unwavering.

"Stay close!" Sophie shouted over the wind, grabbing Tom's hand. "We just need to get to the mountains, and from there, the map says Jack's cave isn't far!"

Tom clutched her hand tightly, trying to fight off the panic rising in his chest. The storm was far worse than anything they had imagined, the wind pushing against them like a wall. But they kept going, one step at a time, their boots sinking deep into the snow.

As they trudged on, the world around them seemed to fade into a blur of snow and wind. There was no sound but the storm—no sign of life, no comforting glow of Christmas lights. Just the endless white expanse stretching in every direction.

After what felt like hours, they reached the foot of the mountains. Sophie pulled out the map, her hands shaking from the cold, but she held it steady. "We're close," she said, her breath forming small clouds in the freezing air. "The cave should be just beyond this ridge."

Tom's legs felt like lead, his cheeks stung from the biting wind, but he nodded, determined to keep going. They scrambled up the rocky incline, their hands slipping on the snow-covered stones, but Sophie's determination didn't waver.

Finally, they reached the top of the ridge—and there it was. Nestled in the side of the mountain, a small, dark cave. Frost clung to the edges of the entrance, and an icy blue light glowed faintly from within.

"That's it," Sophie whispered, her heart racing. "That's Jack Frost's cave."

Tom stared at the cave, fear flickering in his chest. "What if... what if he won't listen?"

Sophie squeezed his hand, offering him a small, reassuring smile. "Then we make him listen. We have to try."

And with that, the two children took a deep breath and stepped forward, heading straight into the heart of winter itself.

## Chapter 7: Sophie and Tom's Search

The wind howled like a living creature, tearing through the snow-covered mountains as Sophie and Tom trudged forward, heads bent low against the biting cold. Snow stung their cheeks, and each step felt heavier than the last, their boots sinking deep into the drifts. The storm showed no mercy.

Tom clutched the worn map of the North Pole in his gloved hands, struggling to keep it from tearing in the fierce winds. The edges were already fraying, the paper flapping wildly, threatening to slip away at any moment.

"I've got this," Tom muttered under his breath, trying to steady himself, his words more a comfort to himself than a declaration. "I've been an Eagle Scout for a while. Map reading should be easy."

But as the snow swirled in violent gusts around them, making visibility nearly impossible, Tom was quickly realizing how wrong he might be. The landmarks that had seemed so clear on the map back in Santa's warm workshop were now lost to the blizzard. The jagged lines of the mountains and valleys were buried under thick blankets of snow, and the tall trees that should have marked the path were nowhere to be seen.

He squinted at the map, turning it this way and that, trying to orient himself in the whiteout. But it was no use. Every direction looked the same—just an endless expanse of snow and wind.

"I think we're going in the right direction," Tom said, but his voice held less confidence than before. The map felt foreign in his hands, like it belonged to a world they were no longer in.

Sophie shot him a doubtful look, her eyes barely visible beneath the hood of her coat. "Are you sure? Because I don't think we've passed any of the spots marked on the map.

And wasn't Jack's cave supposed to be near some tall trees?
I don't see any trees—just more snow."

Tom's stomach churned with frustration, but he didn't
want to admit it. He was supposed to be good at this—navigation, survival skills, all the things an Eagle Scout should
excel at. But out here, in the heart of this relentless storm,
nothing was going the way it should. "Maybe they're just…
covered in snow," he said, though even he didn't believe it.
The trees should have been towering over the landscape,
unmistakable, but all they saw was an endless, blinding
white.

The wind roared louder, cutting through their coats like
icy knives. Sophie pulled her scarf tighter around her face,
her concern deepening with each step. "Tom," she said, her
voice trembling slightly, "maybe we should turn back. This
storm is getting worse, and we don't even know if we're
going the right way."

Tom glanced down at the map again, but the lines blurred
in front of him, the wind nearly tearing it from his hands.
He couldn't deny it anymore—they were lost. His heart
sank, dread pooling in his stomach. The snow was falling
harder now, the drifts piling higher around them. How
could they possibly find Jack's cave in this?

But just as the weight of failure began to settle over them,
something flickered in the distance.

"Tom!" Sophie grabbed his arm, her eyes wide with sudden
hope. "Look! Over there!"

Tom squinted through the wall of snow, barely able to make out what she was pointing at. But there, faint and shimmering, was a blue glow—so faint it was almost invisible, but unmistakable against the stark whiteness of the storm.

His heart quickened. "Do you think that's...?"

"Jack's cave," Sophie whispered, her voice filled with both hope and urgency. "It has to be. Come on!"

Without a second thought, they pushed forward, the cold biting harder at their faces, the snow whipping around them like claws. But the faint glow ahead gave them new strength. They stumbled, slipped, and fought their way through the storm, their legs heavy with exhaustion, but neither of them dared slow down now. The glowing light was their only beacon of hope in the storm's fury.

As they drew closer, the blue light grew stronger, illuminating the snowflakes that danced around them in the wind. It flickered and pulsed, almost like a heartbeat, leading them forward with a quiet, icy pull.

Tom felt his breath hitch in his chest. They were so close. He could feel it.

Sophie's hand tightened around his arm, pulling him faster. "We're almost there!"

Finally, after what felt like an eternity of pushing through the storm, they reached the source of the light. There, nestled between jagged rocks at the foot of a towering snow-covered mountain, was an entrance to a cave. Icicles hung from the edges like frozen daggers, and a soft, ethereal blue light radiated from within, casting an eerie glow on the snow outside.

"That's it," Sophie breathed, her heart racing. "Jack Frost's cave."

Tom stared at the entrance, a mixture of awe and fear swelling inside him. This was it—the source of the storm, the place where Jack Frost was hiding. But now that they were here, standing at the threshold, the enormity of what they were about to do washed over him. Jack Frost wasn't just some mischievous winter spirit. He was a force of nature—unpredictable and powerful.

"What if he won't listen?" Tom asked, his voice small, barely audible above the howling wind.

Sophie, though scared herself, straightened her shoulders. "Then we make him listen. We've come too far to turn back now."

With one last glance at each other, they took a deep breath and stepped forward, entering the icy cave, ready to face the winter spirit and, hopefully, save Christmas before it was too late.

## Chapter 8: Back at the North Pole

Santa sat quietly in his oversized chair, the comforting crackle of the hearth doing little to ease the knot of worry tightening in his chest. Outside, the storm raged on, its relentless howl pressing against the windows like a threat. He watched as Snickel, the lead elf, prepared the search party. The normally bustling workshop had grown tense, the joy of Christmas preparations overshadowed by the children's disappearance.

Snickel stood ready, his small hands trembling slightly as he adjusted the strap on his satchel. Though he tried to keep his focus on the mission ahead, the weight of guilt pressed heavily on his heart.

"I'll make this right, Santa," Snickel said, his voice tight with worry. He avoided looking Santa in the eye, his gaze fixed on the floor. "It's my fault they went after Jack. If I hadn't told them about him..." His words trailed off, and he swallowed hard, as if trying to keep his fears at bay.

Santa, ever patient, watched him for a moment before shaking his head gently. His face, though lined with concern, was soft with understanding. "Snickel," he said, his deep voice warm, "we all make mistakes. You meant no harm, and I've already forgiven you."

But forgiveness wasn't enough to lift the burden from Snickel's shoulders. He fiddled with the edge of his hat, adjusting it nervously, his mind racing with the thought of what could go wrong. "Yeah, but what if I'm on your naughty list now, Santa? What if I've really messed things up this time?" His voice cracked with doubt, and for the first time in his many years of service, he felt like a failure.

Santa chuckled softly, a rich, soothing sound that seemed

to momentarily ease the tension in the room. Despite the dire situation, he couldn't help but be amused by Snickel's fear of the dreaded naughty list. "You won't be on the naughty list, Snickel," he said, his eyes twinkling with the warmth that had made him beloved by all. "You've always had a good heart, and I know you'll do everything you can to fix this. The important thing is that you care, and that makes all the difference."

Still, Snickel couldn't shake the gnawing feeling of dread. He looked out the window at the blizzard, the wind whipping snow against the glass in fierce flurries. The storm had only worsened since Sophie and Tom left, and the longer they were out there, the greater the danger. "I just hope we find them before it's too late," Snickel whispered, his voice barely audible. "I don't know what I'd do if anything happened to those kids because of me."

Santa leaned forward, resting a gentle hand on Snickel's small shoulder. "We'll find them," he said, his voice steady, a quiet strength behind his words. "Go on, Snickel. Lead the search party. You've got this, and you'll bring those children back safely. I believe in you."

Snickel's chest tightened at Santa's faith in him. The guilt still clawed at him, but beneath it, a spark of determination flickered. He couldn't let Santa down. He wouldn't. "I won't let you down, Santa," Snickel said firmly, though his throat felt tight with emotion. "I'll make sure they're safe. I promise."

Santa nodded, his eyes filled with quiet encouragement. "I

know you will."

Snickel turned on his heel, heading toward the group of elves gathered by the door, their bright jackets and gear ready for the search ahead. But as he marched out into the storm, the wind biting at his face and snow already piling high around his feet, Snickel's thoughts kept circling back to the same nagging fear: What if I've really messed things up this time?

He shook the thought from his mind and focused on the task ahead. The cold bit through his coat, and the storm roared in his ears, but Snickel kept moving forward. No, he told himself. Santa always forgives, no matter what. And that was what he clung to as he and the elves began their dangerous trek into the blizzard, searching for Sophie and Tom.

The snow-covered world stretched out before them like an endless white wasteland, but Snickel's determination was fierce. He wouldn't rest until the children were safe, no matter how long it took. Because if there was one thing Snickel knew in his heart, it was that Santa believed in second chances—and Snickel was going to prove that faith was well-placed.

## Chapter 9: Sophie and Tom Nearing the Cave

Through the swirling, merciless storm, Sophie and Tom pushed onward, each step sinking deep into the snow, their faces stinging from the icy wind. The faint blue glow they had seen earlier now grew steadily brighter, flickering like a beacon in the otherwise blinding whiteout. As they neared, the outline of Jack Frost's cave began to take shape, materializing out of the storm like something from a dream—or a nightmare.

But it wasn't at all what they had expected.

The mouth of the cave loomed before them, towering over the snowy landscape like a menacing fortress. At first glance, it almost resembled a castle—but not the kind found in fairy tales. There were no turrets or fluttering flags, no sense of magic or wonder. Instead, jagged spires of ice shot upward into the dark sky, piercing the storm clouds like frozen spears. Each "tower" glittered in the dim, eerie light, as if carved from the coldest, purest ice. The walls of the cave were thick and rough, shimmering with layers of frost and refracting the faint blue glow from deep within.

The entrance itself was a gaping maw, dark and foreboding, framed by enormous icicles that hung like deadly daggers, some so long they nearly scraped the ground. The edges of the cave's opening were jagged and sharp, as if the ice itself had been violently torn apart by the relentless wind that screamed through the canyon.

"It… it looks like a castle," Tom whispered, his breath visible in the freezing air. His eyes were wide with a mixture of awe and fear. "But not like any castle I've ever seen."

Sophie stood beside him, staring up at the towering spires of ice, her heart pounding in her chest. "It's more like an ice fortress," she murmured, her voice barely audible over the howling wind.

Each step forward was met with the soft crunch of snow beneath their boots, the sound seeming louder in the still, frozen air. The chill here was deeper, biting at their skin despite the layers of clothing, and the cold stung their lungs with every breath. The blue light from deep within the cave flickered like something alive, casting long, eerie shadows that danced along the jagged ice walls.

The air felt thick with a strange energy, as though the cave itself was watching them, shifting and breathing with each gust of icy wind. Frost clung to the edges of the walls, glistening like a thousand tiny crystals, whispering secrets from the heart of the mountain.

The wind whistled through the icy spires, creating a high-pitched, ghostly sound that sent chills down their spines. It was as if the fortress itself was alive, watching them, waiting. The spires seemed like frozen sentinels, guarding the entrance to Jack Frost's domain, warning them to turn back.

But they couldn't.

"Do you think he's inside?" Tom asked, his voice small and trembling. His hand instinctively reached for Sophie's, gripping it tightly.

Sophie squeezed his hand back, her breath catching in her throat. She took a deep, steadying breath, trying to muster up courage she wasn't sure she had. "Only one way to find out."

They stepped closer, the blue light from deep within the cave casting a faint glow on the jagged ice walls, creating strange, shifting shadows that danced across the frozen landscape. The cold here was sharper, more intense, as if the very air had been carved from ice. The wind howled louder, echoing through the cave's hollow entrance, making it seem as though the cave itself was breathing.

Sophie felt a shiver run down her spine, not just from the cold, but from the growing sense of foreboding that surrounded them. This wasn't just a cave—it was a place of power, a place where winter itself was born and controlled. Jack Frost wasn't simply a mischievous spirit here; he was the ruler of this frozen domain, and they were trespassing.

With their hearts pounding in their chests, they stood at the edge of the entrance, the darkness inside beckoning them. It was as if the very cave was daring them to step inside.

"We can't turn back now," Sophie said, though her voice trembled slightly. She glanced at Tom, her eyes full of determination, but beneath it, he could see the same fear that gripped his own heart.

Tom swallowed hard, nodding. "Yeah... let's go."

Together, they stepped into the mouth of the cave. The moment they crossed the threshold, it was as if the temperature dropped even further. The cold was biting now, not just on their skin, but in their bones. The wind seemed

to die down outside, replaced by an eerie, otherworldly silence. Only the faint, pulsating blue light from deep within
the cave guided their way.

Inside, the walls of the cave shimmered like glass, reflecting the light in strange, kaleidoscopic patterns. The ground
beneath their feet was slick with ice, forcing them to move
carefully as they ventured deeper into the heart of the cave.
The silence was suffocating, broken only by the sound of
their shallow breathing and the distant, faint hum of the
wind outside.

Sophie's breath hitched. "Tom... do you feel that?"

He nodded, not trusting himself to speak. There was a
presence here, something ancient and powerful, watching
them. The air was thick with magic, the kind that made the
hair on the back of their necks stand on end.

They continued forward, the blue glow growing stronger
with each step. They were close now—closer than ever before. Somewhere ahead, in the heart of this frozen fortress,
was Jack Frost.

And they were about to meet him.

## Chapter 10: Sneaking into Jack's Castle

Sophie and Tom hesitated at the entrance of Jack's icy
fortress, their breaths catching in their throats. The towering, sharp spires of ice seemed to loom over them, casting
long, jagged shadows across the snow. But no matter how
foreboding the castle seemed, they were determined to

go through with their plan. They had come too far to turn back now.

Taking careful steps, they slipped inside, their boots crunching softly on the frozen ground. The moment they crossed the threshold, the temperature dropped even lower. It was as though the very air inside was sharper, colder, more dangerous. Every breath they took felt like it froze in their lungs, sending icy tendrils down their throats.

They kept close to the walls, creeping silently through the narrow passageway. The blue light from the ice walls cast eerie shadows that danced along the floor, making the entire place feel alive, as if the fortress was watching them. The deeper they went, the more the cave transformed into a labyrinth of ice—a fortress of winding corridors and rooms carved from shimmering frost. It was a place of beauty, but also of danger, and the silence pressed down on them like a weight.

They moved slowly, careful not to make a sound, their footsteps barely audible over the soft hum of the ice. The walls glittered with swirling frost patterns, and the ice itself seemed to glow with an otherworldly light. Sophie's heart raced in her chest, every nerve on edge, but she kept pushing forward, glancing back only to make sure Tom was close behind.

Suddenly, they came upon a large chamber, and they both stopped in their tracks.

The room was unlike anything they had ever seen. The

walls sparkled like diamonds, refracting the pale blue light in every direction, making the room glow with a cold, ethereal beauty. In the centre of the chamber stood ice tables and chairs, glistening like they had been carved from the purest glass. Every piece of furniture was intricately detailed—delicate snowflakes etched into the backs of the chairs, swirling frost patterns spiraling across the table-tops.

Sophie's breath caught. "It's... beautiful," she whispered, her voice barely above a breath.

Tom nodded, equally awestruck, but something else caught his eye. In one shadowy corner of the room, perched on a tall, ice-carved stand, was a snowy owl. Its feathers were as white as the snow outside, and its large, golden eyes gleamed in the low light. For a moment, it seemed asleep, its eyes closed, and its head tucked against its chest.

But the instant Sophie and Tom stepped further into the room, the owl's eyes snapped open.

It tilted its head, its glowing golden eyes locking onto the two intruders. The silence in the room suddenly felt suffo-cating, as if the very air had frozen solid.

Before either of them could move, the owl let out an eerie screech, its piercing cry shattering the quiet. The sound echoed through the chamber, bouncing off the ice walls like a haunting, ghostly wail.

Sophie froze, her heart pounding in her chest. Her pulse raced in her ears, drowning out the howl of the wind outside. Tom grabbed her arm, his grip tight, and pulled her behind one of the shimmering ice tables, hoping to hide. But it was too late. The screech had already sounded the alarm.

In an instant, the room seemed to come alive.

From the shadows, figures began to emerge, stepping out of the very walls as if they were part of the ice itself. They moved with silent grace, their bodies shimmering like glass, their skin tinted with the faintest shade of blue. At first glance, they resembled elves, but they were taller—slender and ethereal, their movements smooth and fluid, like the wind. Their eyes glowed faintly in the low light, a cold, icy blue that sent shivers down Sophie's spine.

One of them, taller than the others, stepped forward. His gaze fixed on Sophie and Tom, his eyes narrowing as he surveyed them. His face was sharp and angular, his skin glistening as though it had been dusted with frost. When he spoke, his voice was cold and distant, like the sound of the wind sweeping over a frozen lake.

"Intruders," he said, his voice sending a chill through the room. His gaze pierced through them, unblinking. "What business do you have in the castle of Jack Frost?"

Sophie and Tom stood frozen, their minds scrambling for words. The plan had gone terribly wrong. They had hoped to sneak in, to find Jack Frost and convince him to stop the storm, but now they were surrounded by Jack's icy guards, their exit blocked, their chances of slipping away disappearing like the warmth from their bodies.

Tom swallowed hard, his voice barely a whisper. "We… we're here to—"

"To talk to Jack Frost," Sophie finished, her voice steadier than she felt. She straightened, trying to muster whatever courage she could. "We came to find him," Sophie said, her voice trembling slightly but steady. Her eyes met Jack's, determination flickering despite the fear that crept into her chest. "We need to stop the storm."

Jack's expression flickered, but it was hard to read—like the ice that coated his heart, there was something hidden beneath. His sharp blue eyes lingered on the children for a long moment, and for just a second, the cold in his gaze seemed to soften. "Children, lost in the storm…" he murmured to himself, almost as though he was remembering something distant. His lips curled into a thin, humorless smile. "Curious."

Sophie opened her mouth to speak again, but before she could, the icy figures began to move. In perfect, silent synchronization, they closed in around the two children, their glowing eyes unblinking.

"Take them," the tall guard commanded, his voice colder than the storm outside. "Jack Frost will decide their fate."

Without warning, cold hands grabbed their arms, pulling them forward toward the dark passageway leading deeper into the heart of the fortress. Sophie's stomach lurched, her pulse quickening. This wasn't how it was supposed to go.

Tom shot her a panicked look, but Sophie could only nod, her jaw clenched in determination. They had come to find Jack Frost—and now, it seemed, Jack Frost was about to find them.

## Chapter 11: Jack Frost's Arrival

Jack Frost had been alerted the moment his icy helpers discovered the two young intruders in his fortress. He moved swiftly through the frozen corridors, his long, dark cloak trailing behind him like a shadow, frost spiraling and forming in his wake. The air around him crackled with cold, and the walls seemed to shimmer more brightly as he passed.

As he stepped into the chamber, his presence was immediate, commanding. Sophie and Tom stood frozen in place, surrounded by the tall, glass-like figures of Jack's helpers. The atmosphere was tense, the silence thick with apprehension.

Before either child could finish explaining how they had ended up there, Jack raised a single, icy finger. His expression was calm but unreadable, like the stillness before a winter storm. "Enough," he said softly, his voice as cold and sharp as the wind outside. It carried the chill of winter itself, making Sophie and Tom shiver where they stood.

The room fell deathly quiet. Sophie and Tom exchanged nervous glances, their hearts pounding. They didn't know what to expect from the legendary Jack Frost, but whatever they had imagined didn't come close to the imposing figure before them—cold, distant, and powerful, his very presence commanding the space.

Jack studied the children, his pale blue eyes narrowing slightly. They were just kids—unexpected visitors in his icy domain. In all the years he had been at the North Pole, few had dared venture this far. People usually stayed huddled by their fires, trying to keep warm, far away from the frozen beauty and magic of his realm. The North Pole was something most feared in the heart of winter.

But here were two children, braving the storm, standing in front of him with wide, curious eyes. For a moment, Jack's icy exterior wavered, and something unfamiliar stirred inside him—a flicker of intrigue. He hadn't had visitors, let alone children, in longer than he could remember. He stood frozen himself, caught in the unexpected moment.

Then, a slow smile curled at the edge of Jack's lips, a glint of mischief dancing in his eyes. "Well, well," he murmured, stepping closer to the children. "I suppose you'll need to prove yourselves before I consider anything else."

Sophie and Tom blinked in surprise, their confusion growing. Prove themselves? They hadn't expected this.

Jack's eyes glittered with amusement. "The first task," he announced, his voice carrying a playful edge, "is one of the most important things you can learn when you come to the North Pole: building a snowman."

The room seemed to grow warmer for a moment, as Sophie and Tom processed his words. Building a snowman?

Sophie glanced at Tom, unsure whether to be relieved or more confused.

Tom whispered back, equally puzzled, "Did he just say—?"

But before they could finish their thought, the confusion melted into wide smiles. "Building a snowman!" Sophie whispered excitedly. They loved building snowmen, but they never got much snow at home, and certainly not like this. The idea of playing in the fresh snow, guided by the legendary Jack Frost, made their hearts race with excitement.

Jack's smile broadened as he saw the joy spark in their faces. It was a long-forgotten feeling, one he hadn't experienced in years—the thrill of sharing his love of winter. He had spent so much time alone, ruling over the cold and crafting storms, that he'd forgotten the magic of what winter could mean to others, especially children.

With a wave of his hand, Jack led them through the winding corridors and out of the fortress into a wide-open snowfield. The storm had softened, and the snow glittered under the pale light of the moon, fresh and deep, like a canvas waiting to be painted. The sky above was a muted purple, the stars twinkling faintly in the cold night.

"Let's see what you can do," Jack said, his voice laced with anticipation as he gestured to the endless snow around them.

Sophie and Tom didn't need to be told twice. They dove into the snow with glee, rolling the largest snowballs they could manage. Their laughter echoed through the quiet night as they shaped the snow into the perfect snowman, adding careful details with branches, stones, and snow to bring it to life.

Jack watched them closely, a strange warmth stirring in his chest—a feeling he hadn't known in so long that it almost felt foreign. He stood still, his eyes bright as the children worked, their laughter filling the air. They were creating something with pure joy, and somehow, despite the cold surrounding them, it was contagious. Jack felt it, deep down—a spark of something that had been long buried under years of isolation.

Once the snowman stood proudly before them, tall and perfect, Jack let out a quiet chuckle. "Well done," he said, his voice soft but genuine. "I've seen few snowmen crafted with such care."

Sophie and Tom beamed with pride, their faces flushed from the cold and excitement.

But Jack wasn't done. His mischievous smile returned as he gestured to a nearby pond, the surface of which gleamed like glass under the soft glow of the snow. "And now," Jack said, his eyes twinkling, "we skate."

Without another word, he stepped out onto the ice, gliding effortlessly, as if he were one with the frozen surface. His movements were graceful, almost magical, as he twirled and danced across the shimmering pond.

Sophie and Tom exchanged wide-eyed looks before following him, sliding and laughing as they clumsily skated across the ice. They stumbled at first, but Jack's laughter, light and carefree, echoed around them, and soon they found their rhythm. The three of them glided and spun, their laughter filling the cold night air.

For the first time in a long while, Jack Frost felt truly happy. It was a strange sensation, one he hadn't expected when he first encountered the children. But now, as he skated alongside them, watching their eyes light up with joy, he felt something he hadn't in years—a sense of belonging.

Perhaps winter wasn't meant to be a time of isolation after all.

## Chapter 12: A Day of Fun and Stories

After hours of laughter, sliding down snowy hills, and skating on the glassy pond beneath a pale, glowing moon, Jack led Sophie and Tom back into the warmth of his icy fortress. Their cheeks were red from the cold, and their clothes were damp with snow, but the smiles on their faces told the story of a perfect day. Jack, who had been so distant and cold when they first arrived, now felt a warmth in his chest he hadn't experienced in years. It wasn't just the thrill of sharing winter—it was the simple joy of companionship.

Inside the castle, Jack's icy helpers had prepared a feast fit for the North Pole. The long, ice-carved table was set with plates of steaming food that seemed to defy the freezing air—thick soups that smelled of roasted vegetables and spices, fresh warm bread, and sweet treats dusted with powdered sugar that looked like freshly fallen snow.

Sophie and Tom eagerly sat down, their stomachs rumbling, the excitement of the day making them ravenous. Jack, for his part, took his place at the head of the table, watching with amusement as they devoured everything in front of them. The children's enthusiasm was infectious, and Jack found himself grinning as they tried each dish with delight.

"I haven't had company like this in a very long time," Jack admitted, his voice soft, almost nostalgic. He leaned back in his chair, the pale blue light of the room casting a glow on his sharp features. "It's refreshing."

Once the meal was finished, Jack waved a hand, and the table cleared itself, the dishes vanishing into thin air. Sophie and Tom leaned back in their chairs, full and content, but their eyes were still wide with curiosity. Jack could see it—there was so much they didn't know about his world, so many stories they were eager to hear.

Jack smiled, leaning forward slightly. "Now, how about some stories of the North Pole?" he suggested, his voice carrying the soft cadence of the winter winds, as if the very air around them was infused with magic.

For the next hour, the room was filled with the sound of Jack's voice, weaving tales of snowstorms that danced across the skies, enchanted creatures that lived deep in the heart of the North Pole, and the secret wonders that winter hid from the rest of the world. His eyes sparkled with every word, and Sophie and Tom listened, spellbound, their imaginations painting vivid pictures of the magical world Jack inhabited. He spoke of ancient snow spirits and frozen lakes that held secrets deep beneath their surfaces, of ice caverns filled with crystals that hummed with the music of the wind. It was a world they had never known could exist.

But as the evening wore on, and the glow of excitement began to dim, Sophie's thoughts drifted back to the storm raging outside, the very reason they had come in the first place. She glanced at Tom, and in that silent exchange, they both knew it was time to address the real reason they were there.

Sophie cleared her throat nervously, her heart pounding. "Jack," she began, "this has been amazing. Really. We've never had so much fun in the snow."

Jack smiled warmly, but there was a shift in the air—something heavier, more serious. Sophie's expression turned somber. "But... we need to talk to you about why we're really here. We didn't just come to the North Pole for fun."

Jack's smile faded slightly, his eyes narrowing with curiosity. He leaned back in his chair, his fingers lightly tapping the icy armrest. "Oh?" he said, his voice cool and measured. "And what's brought you to my castle, then?"

Tom shifted in his seat, glancing at Sophie for support before taking a deep breath. "It's Santa," he said, his voice small but steady. "He's in big trouble. His sleigh is broken, there's this huge storm raging outside, and... well, Christmas might not happen this year."

Sophie nodded, her voice taking on a more urgent tone. "And it's my birthday on Christmas Day! My parents took us to Lapland as a special treat, and then... well, we ended up here by accident. But we really need to get back. Not just for me, but for everyone. If Santa can't deliver the presents... Christmas will be ruined."

Jack's expression darkened slightly, his eyes flickering with a trace of emotion. He leaned back further in his chair, his fingers still tapping against the ice. For a moment, he said nothing, letting the weight of Sophie's words hang in the air.

"So... you came all this way to ask for my help?" Jack's voice was quiet but sharp, cutting through the air like the wind outside. His pale blue eyes studied them, his gaze unreadable.

Sophie and Tom exchanged nervous glances. They had hoped to appeal to his better nature, but now, sitting in the presence of this powerful figure, they weren't so sure. "Yes," Sophie said, her voice soft but pleading. "We need your help. We need you to stop the storm... and help Santa. Without you, Christmas might be cancelled, and it'll be all our fault."

The room fell into a heavy silence. Jack's eyes, still cold and distant, flickered with something—something unreadable, a mix of emotions that seemed to war within him. His fingers stopped tapping, and he stared at the children for a long moment, lost in thought.

Sophie and Tom held their breath, waiting.

Jack stood abruptly, his dark cloak billowing slightly as he paced to the far side of the room. His back to them, he spoke slowly, his voice colder now, more distant.    "You think I caused this storm?" Jack's voice was sharp, but there was something beneath it—a tremor that wasn't just frustration but something deeper, something long buried. His fists clenched as frost snaked along the walls, a silent echo of his growing unrest.

Sophie blinked in confusion. "Well... didn't you?"

Jack's fists tightened even more, the frost on the walls thickening. "I didn't summon this storm, Sophie," he murmured, his voice a little quieter now, as if speaking to himself. "It's part of winter's natural course—storms come, whether I command them or not. But when people always assume it's me, when they fear every chill in the air... it feels like it's always my fault."

Sophie's eyes widened in surprise. "But... you can stop it, can't you?"

Jack turned back to face them, his expression hard. "Of course I can. But why should I?"

The question hit Sophie and Tom like a slap of cold air. They hadn't expected that. Tom stammered, "But... Christmas—"

"Christmas," Jack interrupted, his voice heavy with a bitterness they hadn't heard before. "Everyone thinks of Christmas. But does anyone ever think of winter itself? Of me? No. I'm only called when something goes wrong. When the cold gets inconvenient. You only care now because it threatens your holiday."

Sophie's heart raced. She hadn't expected this side of Jack—the loneliness, the resentment. "That's not true," she said, her voice small but earnest. "We came because we need your help. But also, because... you're important too. Winter is beautiful, and so are the things you create."

Jack's gaze softened, ever so slightly, and the frost along the walls seemed to retreat. He watched the children closely, his mind still a whirl of emotions. The silence stretched on again, heavy with uncertainty.

Finally, Jack sighed, the sound echoing softly like the wind. "I'll think about it," he said, his voice quiet but not unkind. He turned away, looking out one of the frost-covered windows, the storm still howling outside. "But not tonight. You two need rest."

## Chapter 13: The Rescue Team Arrives

Just as Sophie and Tom finished their heartfelt plea to Jack, the doors to the icy fortress creaked open. Snickel, leading the rescue team, rushed inside, his breath visible in the freezing air. "We've found them!" he called out, relief evident on his face.

But as he looked around, he quickly realized that everyone

was safe—and perhaps more surprisingly, Jack Frost didn't seem upset. In fact, there was a different air about the room.

"We're here to bring the children back to the North Pole, but it's too late to travel tonight," Snickel said, glancing at the howling storm outside. Snow whipped violently against the fortress walls, and the wind shrieked through the spires of ice. "We'll have to head back in the morning."

Jack stood by the window, his back to them, staring into the blizzard. His hands were clasped tightly behind him, and the frost that had been swirling in the air seemed to hang still for a moment. He nodded slowly. "You're right," he said, his voice quieter than expected. "It's too dangerous to travel now."

He turned to Sophie and Tom, his icy exterior softening, but there was still something hard in his eyes. "After what you've told me, I see now that I've been unaware of the trouble Santa's been having. I knew we had a falling out, but I didn't realize the extent of the problems he's facing." His gaze dropped for a moment, a flicker of pain crossing his face. "I never meant for things to get this bad."

Sophie glanced at Tom. She could feel the tension still hanging in the air like the cold itself. "Jack," she began, stepping forward cautiously, "Santa always said you two were stronger together. He's never stopped hoping you'd come back."

Tom, standing a little behind her, added, "Maybe you

didn't mean for this to happen, but it's not too late to fix it. You can still help."

Jack clenched his fists at his sides, a low crackling sound coming from the ice that laced the walls. The temperature seemed to drop even further, and for a moment, it looked like he might turn away, retreat into the cold and distance that had defined him for so long.

"I…" Jack started, but his voice trailed off. His eyes flashed, caught between guilt and years of stubborn pride. Outside, the wind howled louder, like a mirror to the storm inside him. The frost on the walls thickened, spreading like vines.

Sophie took a deep breath. "Jack, we know you're not the villain here. You just forgot why you were part of Christmas in the first place. It's not about the ice, or the snow, or the storm. It's about helping people—helping Santa."

For a long, silent moment, Jack didn't respond. He turned back to the window, his reflection ghostly in the frost-covered glass. Then, slowly, his fists unclenched, and the ice stopped spreading.

"You're right," he said, his voice barely above a whisper. "I've let it go on too long."

A sigh of relief passed through the room. Sophie and Tom exchanged hopeful looks. The icy tension began to melt, and even the frost on the walls seemed to recede. Jack's shoulders relaxed, and for the first time in years, the cold felt less biting.

Snickel stepped forward, his heart still racing from the earlier panic, but now he felt a wave of gratitude wash over him. "I'm so glad things have been sorted out," he said, bowing slightly toward Jack. "And... well, it seems I owe a lot of thanks to these two," he added, nodding toward Sophie and Tom. "It's clear they've done more to change your mind than I ever could have."

Jack gave a rare smile. "They certainly have."

That night, they all settled in, but the storm outside made for a restless night. The wind screamed through the icy spires of Jack's castle, and now and then, a particularly strong gust made the windows rattle in their frames. Inside, though, there was a sense of calm, as if the thaw in Jack's heart had warmed the air ever so slightly. As they huddled close for warmth, Sophie and Tom whispered about the plans for the morning.

Tomorrow, they would all head back to the North Pole—and Jack would bring his helpers with him. Santa was going to need all the help he could get.

The next morning, as the first light broke through the storm clouds, Jack stood in the centre of the castle, calling his helpers to assemble. They appeared from the shadows, tall and glassy, their bodies formed of shimmering blue ice, each one moving with a graceful, almost liquid smoothness. They didn't speak, but the air around them crackled faintly as they passed, like a frozen breeze on the verge of breaking. Their hollow eyes seemed to glow faintly as they began gathering supplies, their movements swift and efficient, like clockwork beings made of frost.

Jack, Sophie, Tom, Snickel, and the rescue team were ready to leave.

"We've got a long journey back," Jack said, his eyes glinting with determination, the ice-blue colour of his irises almost glowing in the morning light. "But Santa will not face this alone. We'll make sure Christmas is saved."

Snickel nodded, thankful that everything had come together. He watched as Jack led his helpers outside, their ethereal blue forms shimmering against the blinding white of the snow.

The wind had finally calmed, the storm no longer raging against the world. The sky was clear now, and the way ahead looked more hopeful. The children had done what no one else could—they had changed Jack Frost's heart, and now he was ready to help save Christmas.

## Chapter 14: The Journey Back

The journey back to the North Pole was going to be treacherous. The storm had piled snow high into drifts that looked like mountains, while deep valleys carved through the frozen landscape. The snow sparkled in the early morning light, deceptive in its beauty—hiding icy dangers beneath its soft surface. The biting cold gnawed at their faces despite their thick winter gear. Sophie and Tom, bundled tightly in their coats, scarves, and mittens, stared out across the frozen expanse, wondering how they would ever make it through such unforgiving terrain.

But Jack Frost, calm and collected, already had a solution.

Standing tall, Jack drew in a great, deep breath, the icy air swirling around him as his chest expanded. For a moment, everything went still. The wind, which had been howling endlessly, died in an instant. Snowflakes, previously whipped around by the storm, seemed to hang frozen in midair as though the storm itself paused, waiting. Then, with a mighty exhale, Jack blew across the snowy ground, and in a rush of sparkling frost, four shimmering ice sledges materialized before them, forming from the very snow beneath their feet.

Each sledge was a masterpiece, sleek and smooth, carved with intricate frost patterns that swirled like frozen smoke. They gleamed under the pale morning light, reflecting the sun in dazzling shades of blue, white, and silver. The sledges looked like they were crafted from pure crystal, almost too beautiful to touch.

Tom's mouth dropped open as he stared at the creations, his eyes wide with amazement. "Wow..." he whispered, barely able to believe what he was seeing.

Sophie grinned from ear to ear. "Jack, these are incredible!"

Jack, standing tall and proud, couldn't hide his satisfaction. His eyes glinted mischievously as he admired his own handiwork. "Hop on," he said with a sly grin, motioning to the sledges. "We've got a journey ahead of us."

Sophie and Tom scrambled eagerly onto one sledge, Snickel onto another, while Jack took the lead on the front sledge. With a graceful flick of his wrist, Jack sent the sledges shooting forward across the snow. They glided effortlessly, as though the very ice beneath them was helping them along. The wind rushed past Sophie and Tom's faces, cold but exhilarating, and they clutched the sides of the sledge, laughing with delight.

It was like flying.

The world around them blurred as the landscape whipped by, a sea of endless white snow and shimmering ice. For a while, the journey felt like a magical escape, a reprieve from the stress of the storm and their worries about Christmas. Laughter bubbled out of Sophie and Tom as they leaned into the speed, letting the icy wind carry their worries away. Even Snickel, who was usually bogged down with responsibilities at Santa's workshop, couldn't help but smile as he glided across the snow with childlike glee.

But the smooth ride didn't last forever.

Without warning, Jack slowed the sledges, his sharp eyes scanning the ground ahead. A deep, jagged ravine stretched out before them, cutting through the landscape like a wound. The chasm was wide and treacherous, its edges raw from the storm that had torn the ground apart. The snowy terrain on either side had split in two, and the gaping hole descended into an icy abyss that seemed bottomless. The wind whistled eerily as it spiraled down into the darkness below.

The sledges came to a halt at the edge, and the group stared down into the vast chasm, the depth of it making their stomachs drop.

"How are we going to get across that?" Snickel muttered, scratching his head as he peered over the edge, his face scrunched with worry.

Sophie and Tom exchanged uneasy glances, their earlier excitement quickly fading. The gap was far too wide to jump, and there was no way around it. The ravine stretched out for miles, disappearing into the horizon. The path to the North Pole was blocked. Tom looked up at Jack, his voice quiet but filled with hope. "Can you fix this?"

Jack stepped forward, his expression unreadable, his eyes narrowing as he studied the ravine. The cold wind swirled around him, but his face remained calm, as if this were just another part of his endless domain. "Leave it to me," he said confidently, his voice carrying the same quiet power that had mesmerized them from the moment they met him.

He took in another deep breath, the air around him growing colder, frost creeping along the ground in response. Snowflakes began to swirl around his feet, gathering energy from the depths of the winter air. With a powerful exhale, Jack blew across the ravine, sending a gust of freezing wind down into the abyss.

At first, nothing happened. The group held their breath, waiting.

Then, slowly but surely, frost began to gather at the edges of the chasm, crawling outward like fingers of ice. It stretched toward the other side, delicate at first, but growing stronger with every passing second. A bridge began to take shape, piece by piece, each section forming as Jack continued to breathe life into the frozen structure.

The bridge arched high above the ravine, a shimmering masterpiece of pure ice, gleaming in the soft morning light like a crystal highway. It stretched from one side to the other, a delicate yet sturdy path, each step carefully formed with precision. Frost patterns etched themselves along the length of the bridge, intricate and beautiful, as if Jack were signing his name with every icy breath.

After a few more deep breaths, Jack stepped back. The bridge now stood proudly before them, glittering in the sunlight, its surface smooth and perfectly carved, an unbroken connection between the two sides of the ravine.

Sophie's eyes widened in awe, her breath catching in her throat. "Jack, you're amazing!" she exclaimed, her voice filled with genuine admiration.

Snickel, who had been nervously clutching his hat, now let out a sigh of relief. "You're a true master of ice, Jack! This is incredible!" He took a cautious step forward, marveling at the sheer beauty of the ice bridge.

Jack waved off the praise, though a small, satisfied smile tugged at the corners of his mouth. "It's nothing," he said, his voice warm despite the cold around them. "Now let's get moving. Santa's waiting, and we don't have time to waste."

With their path cleared, the group climbed back onto their sledges, one by one, and glided across the ice bridge. The sledges moved effortlessly over the shimmering surface, the bridge holding firm beneath them, its crystalline structure strong and unyielding.

Once they reached the other side, the group pressed on with renewed spirits, their earlier worry replaced by excitement and hope. The North Pole lay ahead, the distant peaks of its snowy mountains just barely visible on the horizon, but now it seemed within reach.

With Jack leading the way, his icy powers clearing every obstacle, Sophie and Tom knew that they would make it. The road was long, and the challenges were many, but with every passing moment, the hope of saving Christmas grew stronger in their hearts.

## Chapter 15: Santa's Dilemma Deepens

The North Pole had never felt so chaotic. With Snickel away leading the search party, the usually well-oiled machine of Santa's workshop seemed to be sputtering. Elves rushed about, their tiny feet pattering across the floor, trying to keep things on track, but without Snickel's steady leadership, the atmosphere was thick with tension. The hum of worry buzzed through the workshop like static in the air.

Over it all, the Christmas clock on the wall—a magical device with 365 digits—continued to tick down the hours with unforgiving precision. Each number glowing brighter as it counted down the minutes until Christmas Eve. Every tick felt louder than the last, echoing through the workshop like the beat of a drum, reminding everyone that time was slipping away faster than they could keep up.

Santa sat by the fireplace, his leg still in a cast from his fall, staring at the clock. The numbers glowed ominously: fewer and fewer hours left until Christmas Eve. His heart was heavy, and his mind raced with worry. The sleigh wasn't fully repaired, the Naughty and Nice list hadn't been updated, and the storm outside showed no sign of easing. Normally, Snickel would have been here to steer the elves, to keep things running smoothly. But now, it was as if the very heart of the workshop had been misplaced.

Santa sighed deeply, rubbing his temples. The weight of Christmas—of disappointing millions of children—pressed down on him like never before. The flames in the fireplace crackled softly, but the warmth felt distant, as though even the fire was beginning to lose hope.

Suddenly, the door to the workshop burst open with a gust of icy wind, causing a flurry of snow to swirl inside. In rushed Nickle, one of Snickel's sons, his breath coming in ragged gasps. He had clearly sprinted all the way from the Christmas Tree Outlook, and his small frame was flushed with urgency.

"Santa!" Nickle shouted, his voice high-pitched with excitement. He nearly tripped over a pile of brightly wrapped presents as he dashed toward Santa, his feet skidding across the floor. "I have news—something's been spotted from the Christmas Tree Outlook!"

Santa sat up straighter, his heart skipping a beat. His eyes, which had been clouded with exhaustion, suddenly sparked with a flicker of hope. "What did you see, Nickle?" he asked, his voice urgent but laced with a cautious optimism. He had been disappointed too many times over the last few days to let hope rise too high too quickly.

Nickle, still panting, stood at attention, his cheeks flushed from the cold outside. "It's big, and it's coming this way fast!" he managed between breaths. "We think it might be... Jack Frost and the search party!"

Santa's heart leaped, a glimmer of hope breaking through the clouds of doubt. "Are you certain?" he asked, his voice rising, tinged with disbelief. Could it really be? Jack Frost— the very being whose presence could turn the tide—coming to help after all?

Nickle nodded so vigorously his little elf hat nearly fell off. "We're positive, Santa! From the speed and the direction, it has to be them!"

For a brief moment, the entire room seemed to freeze. The elves, who had been busy with their frantic tasks, stopped in their tracks. They looked at each other, and then at Santa, their eyes wide with anticipation. The air was thick with the feeling of something about to change, a spark of hope igniting in the faces of even the most exhausted workers.

Santa's eyes lit up, a grin spreading across his face for the

first time in what felt like days. His entire demeanour shifted, as if a great weight had suddenly been lifted. He could
almost feel the cold air outside rushing in, not as a threat,
but as a sign that help was truly on the way. Jack Frost had
been a wild card, but if anyone could clear the storm and
rally the North Pole in time for Christmas, it was him.

"Get ready, everyone!" Santa called out, his voice ringing
with newfound energy. "Prepare the workshop! If Jack
Frost is coming, we'll have the help we need!"

The elves sprang into action, their steps lighter now,
their movements quicker. The tension that had gripped
the workshop seemed to loosen as the news spread, like
the first rays of sunlight breaking through a thick layer of
clouds. Decorations were straightened, toys inspected, and
the unfinished tasks that had been dragging were suddenly
moving forward again with purpose.

Santa watched the flurry of activity with a growing sense of
optimism. His heart felt lighter, the clock ticking down no
longer sounded as ominous. "Come on, Jack," he muttered
under his breath, his eyes gleaming with determination.
"We're counting on you."

As the workshop buzzed with preparation, the storm
outside continued to howl, but now, there was something
different in the air—a feeling of hope. Jack Frost and the
search party were on their way, and if anyone could help
save Christmas, it was the master of winter himself.

## Chapter 16: Sending the Snow Owls

Santa's heart raced with cautious hope, the idea of Jack Frost's arrival flickering like a fragile flame. But years of experience had taught him better than to jump to conclusions. As much as he wanted to believe that Jack and the search party were on their way, certainty was crucial. The storm outside still raged fiercely, and with time running short, there was no room for mistakes. The weight of the ticking Christmas clock, counting down each precious second, pressed heavily on his mind.

Slowly, Santa stood, wincing slightly as he shifted his weight onto his injured leg. His face was lined with determination, even as pain etched into his features. He turned to Nickle, who was standing anxiously by his side.

"We need to be certain," Santa said, his voice thoughtful yet firm. "We can't afford to take any chances."

With that, Santa limped toward the tall cabinet near his desk, where many of his most precious tools and magical artifacts were kept. He reached inside and withdrew a small, silver whistle that gleamed faintly in the light. It was an old instrument, one rarely used, but trusted for moments just like this. Raising it to his lips, Santa blew softly, the sound barely audible to human ears but resonating with magic.

Within moments, two majestic snow owls swooped down from the rafters of the workshop, their white feathers gleaming like freshly fallen snow, dusted with shimmering frost. Their wings spread wide as they hovered, their sharp golden eyes fixed on Santa, awaiting his command.

"Go!" Santa instructed, his voice carrying the urgency of the moment as he pointed toward the stormy horizon. "Find out what's approaching and return with news."

Without hesitation, the owls took off, their powerful wings slicing through the icy wind. They soared out into the night, their white bodies soon vanishing into the thick snow clouds that swirled relentlessly in the storm.

Inside the workshop, tension gripped the air. Every elf stopped in their tracks, their eyes following the owls until they disappeared from sight. The silence was almost un-bearable, punctuated only by the ticking of the Christmas clock. The glowing digits on the wall continued to count down, a constant reminder of how little time remained before Christmas Eve. It felt as though the weight of the entire holiday season was hanging by a thread.

Santa returned to his chair, sinking into it slowly. His leg throbbed, but he ignored the pain, his gaze fixed on the frosted window, watching for any sign of the owls' return. Nickle stood nearby, fidgeting nervously. His eyes darted between the clock and the window, his small hands wring-ing his hat.

"What if it's not Jack?" one of the elves whispered, the fear in their voice echoing the unspoken anxiety in the room.

But Santa silenced the murmurs with a simple wave of his hand. "We'll know soon enough," he said, his voice calm but laced with tension. He knew all too well what was at stake.

The minutes dragged on, each tick of the clock feeling like an eternity. The elves continued to whisper among themselves, their eyes flicking nervously between the clock and the window. Santa's mind raced with possibilities—what if it wasn't Jack Frost? What if the storm was too strong for the search party? What if Christmas truly couldn't be saved this year?

Suddenly, through the howling wind, a soft screech pierced the air. The room collectively held its breath as the familiar shapes of the snow owls glided back through the open doors of the workshop. Their feathers were dusted with ice, but they flew with a graceful precision, landing gently on Santa's desk. Their sharp, intelligent eyes gleamed as they looked directly at Santa, their feathers ruffling as they shook off the frost.

Santa leaned forward, his heart pounding in his chest. "What did you see?" he asked, his voice a soft but urgent whisper.

One of the owls, the larger of the two, ruffled its feathers and let out a low, soft hoot. It then turned its head toward the window, its eyes fixed on something far beyond the frosted glass. Santa, Nickle, and the elves followed its gaze.

At first, they saw nothing but swirling snow, thick and impenetrable, masking the outside world. But then, faintly, through the curtain of falling snow, a glimmer of light appeared. It was dim at first, barely distinguishable from the storm, but it grew brighter, clearer—faint blue lights glowing in the distance, cutting through the darkness like beacons.

Nickle gasped, stepping closer to the window, his breath fogging up the glass. "It is them!" he exclaimed, his voice filled with excitement. "Jack Frost!"

Santa's eyes widened, his heart soaring as hope finally bloomed in his chest. The blue lights in the distance were unmistakable—the telltale sign of Jack Frost's presence. Santa rose from his chair, his leg aching but forgotten in the rush of anticipation. "Prepare for their arrival!" he ordered, his voice filled with a new sense of urgency and purpose. "Jack is coming to help!"

The workshop erupted into action. Elves who had been paralyzed with uncertainty now scrambled to get every-thing ready. Bells rang out, and the sound of hurried foot-steps filled the room as tools were gathered, supplies pre-pared, and the sleigh repair station was brought to life once more. The hum of hope rippled through the air, restoring the energy and focus that had been missing for days.

Santa watched it all unfold, the flurry of activity a welcome change from the gloom that had taken hold earlier. He glanced back at the snow owls, still perched on his desk, their eyes gleaming with quiet intelligence. He gave them a small nod of gratitude, then turned his gaze back to the window, where the faint blue lights continued to glow, growing brighter by the second.

"Come on, Jack," Santa whispered under his breath, his voice filled with both hope and resolve. "We're counting on you."

Outside, the snow continued to fall, but it no longer seemed as menacing. Jack Frost and the search party were on their way, and for the first time in days, Santa truly believed that Christmas might be saved.

## Chapter 17: A Safe Return

As the excitement of the North Pole's grand celebration began to settle, Santa gathered Sophie and Tom near the towering Christmas tree, where elves were bustling about, packing up the final bag of gifts for the sleigh. The storm had passed, leaving the workshop bathed in the soft glow of twinkling lights and the warm hum of last-minute preparations for Christmas Eve. The air was filled with the comforting scents of peppermint and pine, and the quiet clinks of toy parts and wrapping paper rustled softly as elves worked with renewed energy.

Santa, his cheeks rosy and his eyes twinkling like the stars outside, smiled warmly at the children. He leaned on his cane, still healing from his injury, but his spirit was lighter than it had been in days. "You two have done something very special," he said, his deep voice filled with gratitude. "You've helped save Christmas. And for that, I cannot thank you enough."

Sophie and Tom beamed with pride, though a small part of them felt a tinge of sadness knowing their incredible adventure was drawing to a close. They had experienced the magic of the North Pole in a way few ever had. But now it was time to return home.

Jack Frost stepped forward, his breath clouding the air in frosty puffs. His usual mischievous glint was softened, replaced by a more serious, but kind expression. "Now," he said, looking at the children, "it's time to get you both home, but..." He paused, his eyes narrowing playfully. "We can't take you directly."

Sophie tilted her head, her curiosity piqued. "Why not?" she asked, her brows furrowed.

Jack knelt down to their level, snowflakes swirling gently around him as if responding to his presence. His icy blue eyes sparkled with a secret. "If I take you home directly and anyone sees me, it could spoil the magic of Christmas," he explained with a wink. "And we can't risk that, can we? Christmas magic must remain a mystery." He grinned. "But don't worry—I've got a plan."

With that, Jack rose to his full height and led them outside into the crisp, moonlit night. His helpers had prepared a sleek ice sledge, its surface gleaming like crystal under the soft glow of the stars. The sledge was beautiful, etched with delicate frost patterns that shimmered in the cold light.

Sophie and Tom exchanged excited glances as they climbed in, knowing this would be their final ride through the snow. Jack flicked his wrist, and the sledge began to glide smoothly across the snowy landscape, picking up speed as it carried them through the winter wonderland. The snow-covered streets of their hometown came into view, bathed in the soft glow of moonlight. The town was peaceful, almost dreamlike, the world quiet and still under the blanket of snow.

The sledge came to a gentle stop near a small, tucked-away hut hidden among the trees at the edge of town. The hut looked quaint and inviting, with a snow-covered roof and smoke gently curling from its chimney. It was a shelter locals used during snowstorms, a place that would be safe for Sophie and Tom until morning.

"This is as far as I can go," Jack said, stepping off the sledge and helping them down. "You'll be safe here. Rest until morning, and then you can head home." His breath formed frosty clouds as he spoke, the cold air swirling around them like a protective shield.

Sophie and Tom stood in the quiet of the night, the snow crunching softly beneath their boots. They looked up at Jack, their hearts warm despite the cold. Jack smiled down at them, a mixture of pride and something more—a fondness for the children who had reminded him of the true magic of Christmas.

"I can't go any further," Jack said softly, his voice carrying the gentleness of falling snow. "But I want to wish you both a very happy Christmas when it comes. And I hope you get everything you've wished for."

Sophie's heart swelled with emotion, and she stepped

forward, wrapping her arms around Jack's waist in a tight hug. "Thank you, Jack," she whispered, her voice filled with gratitude.

Tom, following his sister's lead, hugged Jack too, his face bright with the joy of everything they had experienced. "Yeah, thank you, Jack. For everything."

Jack knelt down one last time, his icy fingers tipping the brim of his hat with a playful grin. "No, thank you," he said, his eyes twinkling like the stars above. "You've reminded me just how important Christmas really is."

With one final, sweeping bow, Jack rose to his feet and stepped back into the sledge. The wind picked up, swirling snow around him as he gave them a final nod. Then, with a gust of icy wind and a flick of his wrist, Jack disappeared into the night, the sledge vanishing into the swirling snow as though it had never been there at all.

Sophie and Tom stood in the moonlit snow, watching until the last flicker of Jack's icy magic faded into the night. The world around them was silent, save for the soft sigh of the wind through the trees. They turned to each other, still buzzing with the magic of the North Pole, the adventure lingering in their hearts like the warm glow of a Christmas fire.

"We did it," Tom whispered, smiling as they headed toward the cozy hut, its warmth inviting them inside.

"Yeah," Sophie agreed, her voice soft but filled with wonder. "And we'll never forget it."

The door of the hut creaked open as they stepped inside, the warmth enveloping them. They settled down, their hearts still racing with the excitement of the journey. As they rested, they knew that when morning came, they would return to their normal lives, but the magic of what they had experienced would stay with them forever.

And somewhere, in the heart of winter, Jack Frost smiled, knowing that Christmas had been saved—and that the magic of the season was as alive as ever.

## Chapter 18: Found in the Snow Hut

As Sophie and Tom slept soundly in the small snow hut at the edge of town, their breath rising in soft clouds of warmth, the outside world was still wrapped in worry. Their parents, along with neighbors and members of the search party, had been scouring the snow-covered streets for hours. The entire town had been searching frantically, calling out for the children through the storm, their voices echoing through the empty night, but to no avail.

Snow crunched underfoot as the weary searchers made their way back through the trees. Their faces were drawn with exhaustion, eyes wide with worry, every step weighed down by fear of what they might—or might not—find. As the group trudged through the snow, one of the neighbors paused, his eyes narrowing as he looked toward the little hut nestled between the trees.

"Maybe we should check the snow hut again," he suggested, his voice tight with concern. "It's worth a look."

Sophie and Tom's father, his face etched with lines of worry, glanced up. His breath puffed out in white clouds as he nodded. "Yes," he said, his voice rough with exhaustion but laced with a glimmer of hope. "We'll try anything."

The group quickened their pace, hearts pounding as they reached the small wooden door of the snow hut. Slowly, Sophie and Tom's father pushed it open, holding his breath as the hinges creaked. Inside, bathed in the soft glow of the moonlight filtering through the small window, were the two children—curled up together under thick, warm blankets, fast asleep.

For a moment, there was only silence, a stunned pause as everyone took in the sight.

Then, a collective sigh of relief rippled through the group, the tension in the air dissolving like snow under the sun. Sophie and Tom's mother let out a joyful cry, rushing forward. "They're here!" she called, her voice breaking with emotion. "They're safe!"

The rest of the search party hovered near the door as their mother knelt beside them, gently brushing the snow from their boots and stroking their hair. Their father followed, his hand trembling slightly as he knelt down and touched Tom's shoulder.

"Wake up, my darlings," their mother whispered, her voice soft and full of love. "It's time to go home."

Sophie stirred first, blinking sleepily as her eyes adjusted to the dim light of the hut. Tom stretched beside her, rubbing his eyes with the back of his hands, still wrapped in the warmth of the blankets. But as soon as they saw their parents' faces, the memories of their incredible adventure came rushing back in vivid detail.

"We were at the North Pole!" Sophie exclaimed, sitting up suddenly, her heart still racing with excitement. She glanced at Tom, her wide-eyed look mirrored on her brother's face.

"And Jack Frost took us there!" Tom added eagerly, his voice full of wonder. "He made us these amazing ice sledges, and we flew across the snow! It was so cool!"

Their parents exchanged confused glances, smiling but clearly uncertain. The story tumbled out of Sophie and Tom, their words overlapping as they tried to recount everything at once—about Santa, Jack Frost, the ice sledges, and the magical adventure to save Christmas. They were animated, full of energy, as if they had just returned from the most magical place in the world.

But their parents only smiled softly, brushing the hair from their children's foreheads. "It sounds like you've had quite the dream," their father said gently, his voice filled with warmth but disbelief.

Sophie's eyes widened. "But it wasn't a dream!" she insisted, glancing at Tom for support. "It really happened! Jack Frost is real!"

Their mother chuckled, kissing the top of Tom's head. "It must have been a wonderful dream," she said tenderly. "You've had quite the night, haven't you?"

The rest of the search party nodded in agreement, murmuring softly about children's imaginations and how vivid dreams could feel so real. But as they gently wrapped the blankets around Sophie and Tom and prepared to head home, the children exchanged a glance—one that held a shared secret, a look of understanding that only they could truly grasp.

To the adults, it may have been a dream—a fanciful tale woven in the safety of a snow hut. But Sophie and Tom knew the truth. Deep down, they could still feel the rush of the icy wind on their faces, the sensation of flying on the ice sledges, the warmth of Santa's smile, and Jack Frost's playful, knowing grin.

As they walked through the snowy night, bundled in their parents' arms, Sophie and Tom shared a quiet smile. The snow fell gently around them, and the magic of the North Pole lingered in their hearts like a cherished secret. Dream or not, they knew they had been part of something extraordinary—an adventure that no one else could ever truly understand.

And in the soft stillness of the night, just beyond the edge of the trees, a faint glimmer of blue light flickered in the distance, disappearing as quickly as it had appeared.

Sophie and Tom smiled to themselves. They knew Jack

Frost was still watching, ensuring the magic of Christmas lived on.

## Chapter 19: Christmas Eve in Lapland

Later that day, after the search had ended and the family was safely reunited, Sophie and Tom returned with their parents to the cozy chalet they had rented in the heart of Lapland. The cabin was a picture-perfect Christmas hideaway, with its wooden beams draped in garlands and a tall Christmas tree twinkling with lights by the window. The soft glow of candles and festive decorations filled the room with warmth, making it feel as though the holiday spirit had woven itself into every corner.

Outside, the air was crisp and cold, the snow falling gently in soft, shimmering flakes. The sound of Christmas carols drifted through the streets as locals gathered in small groups, their voices harmonizing in cheerful melodies. The scent of pine and cinnamon wafted through the air, mixing with the comforting crackle of the fire burning in the hearth. It was Christmas Eve, and the world felt alive with anticipation.

Sophie and Tom sat near the fire, their cheeks still rosy from the cold outside, their eyes reflecting the flickering flames. The warmth of the cabin wrapped around them like a blanket, but their thoughts were far away—drifting back to the magical adventure they had just returned from. They could still feel the cold, biting air of the North Pole, the sleek smoothness of Jack Frost's ice sledges beneath their hands, and the gentle hum of magic that seemed to hang in the air around Santa's workshop.

In their minds, they could still see the towering spires of Jack's icy castle, the blue lights that glowed against the snow, and the laughter of the elves echoing through the snowy hills. It felt like a dream, but Sophie and Tom knew better. Every detail was etched in their memories, more vivid than any dream they had ever had.

Their parents, unaware of the grand adventure their children had been a part of, smiled softly as they watched Sophie and Tom nestled by the fire. To them, the children seemed quieter than usual—more reflective, perhaps—but the joy in their faces was undeniable. It was as if some extra layer of magic had wrapped itself around this Christmas, making it feel warmer, brighter, and more meaningful than any they had experienced before.

Sophie caught Tom's eye, and they exchanged a knowing glance—one of those shared, secret smiles they had given each other ever since their return. It was the smile of two children who had seen something no one else could understand, who had shared in something so magical and extraordinary that it almost seemed too good to be true.

Their hearts bubbled with excitement as they thought about what Christmas morning might bring. After everything they had been through—the ice sledges, the North Pole, and the moment they helped save Christmas—it felt like anything was possible. They knew that this Christmas was different. It wasn't just about the presents or the tree or even the carols. It was about something much bigger:

the magic that could be found if you just believed.

As they sat by the fire, their thoughts wandered back to Jack Frost. They imagined him out there somewhere, weaving through the winter sky, watching over the snow-covered land with that mischievous smile on his face. Maybe, just maybe, he'd pay them another visit someday. But even if he didn't, they knew they'd carry the magic of that adventure with them forever.

Their parents, still watching from across the room, couldn't help but feel a sense of wonder themselves. They didn't know what it was—perhaps the beauty of the snow, or the warmth of the cabin, or the glow on their children's faces— but this Christmas felt special. It felt like something magi- cal was in the air, just out of reach, whispering through the falling snow.

Sophie and Tom snuggled deeper into their blankets, the glow of the fire making them drowsy but content. As they closed their eyes, their thoughts danced with the memories of their adventure. They were sure of one thing: this would be a Christmas they would never forget.

And outside, in the snowy hills just beyond the town, a faint gust of wind stirred the trees. If anyone had been looking, they might have noticed a trail of delicate, frosty patterns winding through the air—there for just a moment before disappearing into the winter night.

## Chapter 20: Christmas Morning Magic

Christmas morning arrived in Lapland, and the air was

alive with excitement. Sophie and Tom were up before the first light of dawn, their hearts racing as they bounded downstairs. The cozy chalet was bathed in the warm glow of the Christmas tree, its lights twinkling like tiny stars. The smell of fresh pine mixed with the inviting aroma of hot chocolate that wafted through the room, adding to the festive charm.

Their parents were already sitting by the fire, steaming mugs of hot chocolate in their hands, smiling as they watched the children dash toward the tree. After all the excitement of the past few days, Sophie and Tom had slept soundly, their dreams filled with memories of the North Pole. But now, the magic of Christmas morning had taken over, and they were eager to see what surprises awaited them under the tree.

"Good morning!" their mother called out, her voice full of warmth and cheer. "Looks like Santa was busy last night."

Sophie and Tom exchanged a knowing glance, their eyes twinkling with a secret they both shared. They hadn't spoken much about their adventure to the North Pole since returning, but the magic still lingered between them, a shared spark that made this Christmas feel more special than ever.

They darted toward the pile of presents, tearing into the colourful wrapping paper with glee. Laughter echoed through the cabin as they unwrapped dolls, books, and toys, each new gift met with gasps of delight. The tree was surrounded by crumpled paper and ribbons, and the children's joy filled the room like the glow of the morning sun.

But then, something caught Sophie's eye.

At the very back of the tree, hidden behind the other gifts, were two small presents. Unlike the others, these weren't wrapped in the usual festive paper. They seemed to shimmer with a soft glow, sparkling in the warm light of the Christmas tree as though they held a secret all their own.

"Hey, look at these!" Sophie said, her voice filled with awe as she pointed to the hidden gifts. "They're special!"

Tom crawled over, eyes wide with curiosity. He reached out and grabbed one of the boxes, feeling the cool, smooth paper that almost seemed to hum with magic. "Who are these from?" he asked, glancing at his parents.

Their parents exchanged puzzled looks. "We didn't put those there," their father said, sitting up straighter in his chair. "Did you?"

Their mother shook her head, her brow furrowing in confusion. "No... I didn't," she replied softly, her eyes now fixed on the glowing gifts.

Sophie and Tom, their hearts pounding with anticipation, carefully unwrapped the mysterious presents. As the paper fell away, they revealed two beautiful snow globes nestled inside the boxes. The globes shimmered with a soft, magical light, and when Sophie and Tom held them up, their breath caught in their throats.

Inside each globe was a tiny, perfect scene of the North Pole. Santa's workshop stood tall, surrounded by glittering snow-covered hills. The reindeer pranced in midair, pulling the sleigh in graceful circles, while tiny elves danced and laughed around a sparkling Christmas tree. And there, in the distance, stood Jack Frost's ice castle, its spires shimmering in the swirling snowflakes.

Sophie's eyes widened with wonder as she gently shook her snow globe, sending a flurry of glittering snow cascading down over the scene inside. "It's just like it was," she whispered to Tom, her voice barely audible over the crackling of the fire.

Tom nodded, equally mesmerized. "It's perfect," he said softly, his eyes locked on the swirling magic inside the glass.

Their parents, still watching from the sidelines, leaned forward, their curiosity piqued. "Where did these come from?" their mother asked, her voice filled with wonder. "Who are they from, children?"

Sophie and Tom shared another smile, that same secretive grin they had been exchanging since their return. They knew exactly who the snow globes were from. They knew the truth behind the magic.

"Santa Claus," they said in unison, their voices filled with certainty and joy.

Their father chuckled softly, shaking his head with amusement. "Santa Claus, huh?" he said, exchanging a quizzical look with their mother. "Well, he certainly has a way with surprises."

Their mother smiled, though her expression was still one of mild confusion. "They are beautiful," she admitted, her eyes tracing the delicate details of the snow globes. "Maybe Santa really did leave them."

Sophie and Tom hugged their snow globes close, their fingers tracing the smooth, cool glass, but the warmth they felt didn't come from the glow of the fire. It came from something deeper, something that pulsed in their chests with every beat of their hearts. They had seen the North Pole. They had saved Christmas. They had stood beside Jack Frost, and the memory of that magic would live within them forever, like a spark of frost that would never melt.

"It's real, isn't it?" Sophie whispered, her voice barely audible as she gazed at the swirling snow inside her globe.

Tom smiled softly, his breath fogging the glass for a moment. "Yeah. It's real. And no one can ever take that from us."

Their parents might not have believed the story, and maybe no one else ever would, but Sophie and Tom knew. They would carry the secret of the North Pole with them for the rest of their lives, a hidden warmth they could always return to, no matter how cold the world around them might be.

As their parents sat back, sipping their hot chocolate and watching the children with soft smiles, the room seemed to hum with the gentle magic of Christmas morning. The snow outside fell quietly, blanketing the world in a peaceful stillness, while inside, the warmth of family and the wonder of the season wrapped around them like a cozy embrace.

It had been a Christmas like no other—a Christmas filled with wonder, magic, and the kind of adventure only Sophie and Tom could truly understand. And as they watched the snowflakes swirl inside their magical snow globes, they knew that this Christmas would stay with them, shimmering in their memories like the glittering snow of the North Pole.

## About Me

I was born in Scotland and have lived here all my life. For thirty years, I worked in the North Sea for Marathon Oil, a unique and amazing environment that always reminded me of how special the world is. During my time at sea, I would make up stories for my two boys, spinning wild tales about the places I had been. One of their favourites was the story about six-foot-tall seagulls with attitude!

I've always been a dreamer, and my first love was art. I am self-taught in digital art techniques and love using computers to create various pieces of artwork. My vivid imagination and creative spirit continue to inspire my storytelling today.

Sophie    Santa    Jack Frost    Tom

www.ingramcontent.com/pod-product-compliance
Lightning Source LLC
Chambersburg PA
CBHW072032150726
47999CB00002B/867